SPORT STORIES

FOOTBALL SURPRISE

TEXT BY EMMA CARLSON BERNE

ILLUSTRATIONS BY KATIE WOOD

Raintree is an imprint of Capstone Global Library Limited, a company
incorporated in England and Wales having its registered office at 264
Banbury Road, Oxford, OX2 7DY   Registered company number: 6695582

www.raintree.co.uk
myorders@raintree.co.uk

Text © Capstone Global Library Limited 2017
The moral rights of the proprietor have been asserted.

Graphic Designer: Heather Kindseth
Production Specialist: Michelle Biedscheid
Illustrated by Katie Wood
Originated by Capstone Global Library Ltd
Printed and bound in China

ISBN 978 1 4747 3230 7
20 19 18 17 16
10 9 8 7 6 5 4 3 2 1

British Library Cataloguing in Publication Data
A full catalogue record for this book is available from the British Library.

Every effort has been made to contact copyright holders of material
reproduced in this book. Any omissions will be rectified in subsequent
printings if notice is given to the publisher.

CONTENTS

CHAPTER ONE

A NEW POSITION

Tweeet! The referee's whistle rang out across the football field. It was the start of the second half against the Hornets.

After an uplifting halftime talk by Manager Mike, the Strikers were feeling good. They were only down by one goal.

As a midfielder, Alex had to be ready. Her eyes were on the ball in the centre of the field. She was ready to kick it as soon as it came her way.

Alex had moved to Riverside last month. This was her first game with the Strikers. The team was undefeated so far. They only needed to win two more games and they'd go to district finals.

On her old team, Alex was a forward. She loved being a forward and was having a tough time being a midfielder.

Alex felt an unexpected pain in her throat at the thought of her old team, the Tiger Moths. She had known most of those girls since junior school. Her two best friends, Mia and Stella, were the other two forwards.

Alex had cried for a week when her mum told her they were moving. She didn't need to start up again now in the middle of a game.

Alex knew she was better on attack. She just needed a chance to prove herself. Manager Mike would be sure to move her to centre forward once he saw her skills.

The score was 1-0. The Hornets were up. The Strikers needed to score in the next few minutes to draw the game level. Then the game would go into extra time.

Alex looked around, catching the eye of Lin. Lin was a defender. Alex and Lin had become good friends in the last month.

"Come on, Strikers!" Alex shouted encouragingly. "Let's go, girls!"

Lin shouted, "Let's go, Strikers!"

The purple-shirted Hornets were quickly dribbling the ball down the field. They were easily moving around the Strikers' defence.

Alex could see the concentration on their faces. The Hornets' centre midfielder looked right and left. Then she made a quick pass to one of the forwards. Lin was ready and stole the ball quickly.

"Alex!" Lin shouted.

Alex signalled that she was open. Lin passed her the ball. Alex gained control immediately. She dribbled down the field.

Alex passed the ball to Brooke, the Strikers' centre midfielder. But in an instant, the Hornets' defence was on her.

"Here, Brooke!" yelled Nadia, one of the Strikers' forwards. She waved her arms. "I'm open!"

Brooke turned, saw Nadia and passed her the ball. The black-and-white sphere shot across Alex's field of vision.

Without thinking, Alex fell back into the role of a forward. She intercepted the ball. In a quick one-two dribble, Alex ran towards the goal. The field seemed like a blur.

The net was wide open, the goalie running back into place. Alex kicked the ball into the goal.

Smack! Nothing was as satisfying as that sound of her foot against the ball.

The ref's whistle blared. Then he shouted, "Own goal! Goal for Hornets!"

Alex looked around, confused. Then she saw the colour of the goalie's jersey and the shocked faces of her teammates.

Alex realised that she hadn't saved the Strikers at all. In fact, she'd kicked the ball into the wrong goal.

As the Hornets celebrated their win, the Strikers sadly walked off the field.

"I guess you forgot which team you were playing for," Brooke said to Alex. Then she walked away.

CHAPTER TWO

A SIMPLE MISTAKE

Alex couldn't move. She felt frozen to the field. She was aware of the players leaving the field. Everyone was lining up for the post-game handshakes. She still couldn't believe what she had done!

Over by the stands, parents were packing up blankets and lawn chairs. It seemed like everything was in slow motion.

"Okay, team! Huddle up!" Manager Mike said.

Alex sank onto the grass beside the rest of the Strikers. The shock of what had just happened was beginning to wear off. She felt like she could think more clearly now. Scoring like that was an accident, of course.

She looked around at her teammates. They were all slumped on the grass. Alex swallowed. Everyone looked really bummed. Some girls even looked mad.

They can't be mad, Alex thought. *It was a mistake. It happens to everyone.*

"Okay, girls," Manager Mike began, hands on his hips. "This is our first loss of the season. It's a bummer."

"It's more than a bummer," Brooke said, shooting a mean look towards Alex. "Now we have to work extra hard to make playoffs."

"It wasn't our best game. But we had some really nice passing out there and some excellent aggressive play when attacking," Manager Mike said encouragingly. "You all gave it heart, and I'm proud of you."

He paused and glanced at Alex. Then he went on, "Now, some of you are still learning, and that's fine. Practise makes perfect."

"Whatever," Brooke said.

Alex just stared at the grass. He didn't mean her, did he? That didn't make sense. She wasn't still learning. She had been playing football since she was four! It was a simple mistake.

If I was still a forward, none of this would have happened, Alex thought.

Brooke got to her feet, her blond ponytail bobbing up and down. Beside her, Lin sat quietly, looking down at her lap.

"Sir, I think there is someone on this team who really messed up today," Brooke said, staring at Alex. "I think she should apologise."

Alex felt her face burn as everyone stared at her. Apologise? For a simple mistake? Brooke was crazy. But everyone else was nodding. Even Manager Mike seemed to be waiting for her to say something. The silence stretched out.

Finally, Alex took a deep breath. "Um, I know I kicked the ball into the wrong goal," she said. "But that was a total mistake. It could happen to anyone. I'm just used to being a forward."

Her words sounded a little more defensive than she'd intended. She looked around for support but instead saw only angry faces.

A wave of confusion swept over Alex. Obviously she hadn't meant to score for the other team. Couldn't anyone understand that? Alex looked around. Only Lin looked sympathetic.

Manager Mike spoke up. "All right, players, let's call it a day," he said. "It was a tough game, and I think we all need some rest. See you all at practice tomorrow."

Everyone started gathering their things and heading towards the car park. Alex took a while finding her water bottle. When she got to her feet, she found she was alone on the sidelines.

She walked towards her mum's car and caught a glimpse of Lin, disappearing into her parents' car.

"Lin, wait up!" Alex called, running towards her.

Lin turned around. "Uh, sorry, Alex, got to go!" she called back. "Dentist appointment. See you tomorrow."

Alex slowed down, dragging her boots through the gravel. She wasn't looking forward to the car ride home.

CHAPTER THREE

LONG DRIVE HOME

Alex climbed into the minivan and slammed the door. After buckling her seat belt, she slumped low in her seat. She propped her boots on the dashboard as her mum pulled out of the parking lot.

"Now, hon–" Mum began right away. She glanced at her daughter and said, "Alex Hausman! I've told you a thousand times not to put your feet up there."

Alex sighed and thumped her feet to the floor. Her mum continued, "I know you're probably feeling bad about that goal, but everyone makes mistakes. I'm sure it's happened to some of the other girls before."

"Mum, that's not it!" Alex said, pushing herself up in the seat. "I told them all it was just a mistake, and everyone just stared at me."

"They were probably upset about losing their first game," Mum said. "Give them a little time." She glanced over at Alex. "But honey, you know you are defence. What were you doing trying to shoot anyway?"

Alex stared at her lap. "I forgot. I'm so used to being a forward. I just wanted to help out my new team," she mumbled, twisting her fingers. "Anyway, I should be attacking. I was back home."

Mum steered the car into their driveway and turned off the engine. She sat for a moment, staring out through the windshield at their tidy brick house.

"Alex," she said softly. "I know this move has been hard on you, but this is home now. And everyone here is going to see what a great player you are. You need to prove yourself and gain their trust."

Alex picked at a loose thread on her shiny football shorts. "I feel dumb stuck at midfield," she mumbled. "No one here knows I used to be an awesome forward."

Mum patted her knee. "Maybe not," Mum said. "But that was in the past. Now you're a midfielder."

Alex stared straight ahead through the windscreen.

"Alex, it doesn't matter what position you play. Just have fun," Mum said cheerfully. She got out of the car. "I made beef stew for tonight. Doesn't that make you feel a little better?" she asked.

"Yeah, thanks, Mum," Alex managed to reply.

But as she followed her mother into the house, she thought that the only thing that would make her feel better would be forgetting this day ever happened.

CHAPTER FOUR

BAD TO WORSE

The next afternoon, Alex walked onto
the field with determination. The bright
sunshine and light breeze tossing the
treetops made her feel as if the incident
yesterday had never happened. Mum was
right. Everyone else had probably already
forgotten about it, too.

Most of the Strikers were already on the
field, kicking balls from one to the other or
stretching on the sidelines.

Duffel bags and footballs were scattered on the grass. Manager Mike was sitting on the bench looking at his clipboard.

Alex dumped her bag next to the others and hurried over to Lin and Brooke, who were passing a ball back and forth.

"Hi guys," she greeted them cheerfully.

"Hi," Lin said back, and passed the ball to Brooke. But Brooke just narrowed her eyes and looked away.

Alex's mouth fell open. Was Brooke actually still mad about yesterday? She looked back at Lin, who gave a little shrug.

Alex opened her mouth to say something to Lin, but before she could, Manager Mike called, "Okay, players, get into position for drills!"

Brooke was just being crabby, Alex decided as she took her place in one of the two double lines. She tried to catch the eye of Christie, her passing partner, but Christie just frowned and looked away.

Alex swept her eyes over the two lines of girls passing the ball back and forth. No one looked at her. In fact, it seemed like everyone was ignoring her. There was a definite tension in the air.

Alex kicked the ball back to Christie as hard as she could. *They can't forgive one mistake?* she thought. *They are just stuck-up, that's all. The Tiger Moths never would have treated me like this.*

Alex's stomach churned uneasily as the practice dragged on. After drills they played a match. Alex was not surprised when nobody would pass her the ball.

At the end of practice the manager gave a pep talk about the upcoming game.

"We lost a tough game yesterday," Manager Mike said. "But I know we're ready to win big tomorrow. I'll see you all here at four o'clock sharp. Everyone get a good night's sleep."

The girls broke up, huddling in little groups as they packed up their gear. Alex grabbed her bag and hurried over to the bench, where Lin was changing her boots for a pair of trainers.

"Hey, Lin!" Alex said. "Do you want to come over? My mum can drive you home later."

Lin seemed uncomfortable. A couple of girls nearby looked at Lin, waiting to hear her answer.

Lin finished tying her shoes and grabbed Alex's arm. She pulled her off to the side of the field. A couple of tall bushes provided a handy screen as Lin leaned in close.

"Listen, Alex, I have to talk to you," Lin whispered. She shifted a little. "Everyone's still kind of mad about yesterday."

"I cannot believe this!" Alex exclaimed, her voice rising. "One tiny mistake and I'm going to be blamed for the rest of the season!" She crossed her arms. "Look, I'm sorry it was the first loss, okay?"

"Calm down, Alex," Lin whispered, making patting motions with her hands. "It's not that it was the first loss, exactly."

"Then what's the problem?" Alex asked.

"It's just that, well, some of the girls feel like you should say you're sorry," Lin said. "Even if it was just a mistake. You are being kind of rude about the whole thing."

"If anyone is being rude, it's not me," Alex replied angrily. "And I suppose you think I should apologise, too?"

Alex didn't know why she was getting mad at Lin. Lin was just trying to help her. But she felt like she had to get mad at someone.

"Well. . ." Lin looked down and scuffed the gravel with her feet. "I guess, yeah. That is what I think. I think you should say you're sorry."

"Well, I don't," Alex snapped and stomped away.

CHAPTER FIVE

PULL IT TOGETHER

Her mum was standing over the stove when Alex snuck in the back door. She walked fast through the kitchen, hoping she could make it to the stairs before Mum saw her red eyes.

"Hey, Alex," Mum said behind her. "How was practice?"

"Fine," she said in what she hoped was a casual voice.

"What's wrong, honey?" Mum asked as she sat down on a high stool at the kitchen island. She patted the seat next to her.

Alex sighed and sat on the stool next to her mum. She propped her head on her arm.

"Mum, I just don't know what to do!" she said. "The team's totally mad at me. Lin says they all want me to say I'm sorry for scoring for the other team. And I want to, but I feel so stupid now because it's been too long. And they're all going to hate me forever, and I'll never have any friends here. This place is awful! This never would have happened back at home." A couple of tears spilled down her cheeks.

Her mum rubbed Alex's back, the way she used to when Alex was little.

"The girls can't stay mad forever. Your next game is tomorrow, right?" her mum asked.

Alex nodded.

"Just make sure you're the best team player out there," Mum said. "Don't move one step outside of your position, pass to everyone, play hard and play fair. That's what made you such a good teammate on the Tiger Moths, and that's what will make you one on the Strikers."

She returned to stirring the sauce and said, "I wish I could be there tomorrow, but I have a work meeting. But I'll be thinking of you. You can do it, Alex."

"Thanks, Mum," Alex replied. "I'll do my best."

Alex trailed out of the kitchen. She was exhausted. Back in her room, she dropped her duffel bag on her bed and stared in the mirror over her dresser. She had puffy eyes and messy hair. She looked terrible.

"I need to pull it together. Play hard, play fair," she said to herself out loud. "I can do this."

CHAPTER SIX

THE PASSING PROBLEM

"Okay, Strikers, look alive!" Manager
Mike called from the sidelines the next
afternoon. He stood with his hands on his
hips. He hoped his team was ready.

Out on the field, the Strikers were ready
for the kickoff against the Thunder. Brooke
was facing off against a tall girl with braces
and a brown ponytail.

Back in her new position, Alex crossed
her fingers and took a deep breath.

No one had talked to her as they'd arrived for the game, but her mum was right. She wasn't a Tiger Moth anymore. She was a Striker now, and she had to adjust. Alex needed to be a better team player.

Tweeeet! The ref's whistle sounded. Brooke and the Thunder's centre fought for the ball. Brooke gained control. The parents on the sidelines cheered loudly as she swiftly dribbled towards the goal.

A Thunder defender was on her, but she passed to the left. Nadia captured the ball, ducking around a Thunder defender, and shot at the goal.

The Thunder's goalie slid left and caught the ball with her arms outstretched over her head.

The players fought for position as the Thunder's goalie threw the ball towards the tall centre. The centre easily blocked the ball, whipping around and dribbling fast down the field. The Thunder's manager yelled and jumped up and down on the sidelines.

The girl came closer, and Alex tensed for action. Christie ran up to the girl and stole the ball. Alex saw her looking around for someone to pass to. This was her chance!

"Here, Christie!" she yelled, jumping up and waving her arms. But Christie glanced over and looked away fast. She passed instead to Brooke, even though she had two Thunder defenders marking her.

Why didn't Christie pass to me? Alex wondered. She was way closer and more open than Brooke.

But Alex didn't have time to think about the situation for very long. The Striker centre had regained control of the ball again and was dribbling towards her, fast.

Alex swooped in front of the girl, neatly stealing the ball. Then, as carefully as she could, dribbled forwards and passed to Nadia. There. She breathed a tiny sigh of relief.

The whole team had seen her stay in position and start an attack, just like she was supposed to.

But her teammates must not have noticed. Just before halftime, another forward, Marissa, was taking a corner. Alex positioned herself for the ball, but Marissa looked at her and looked away. She passed straight to Christie, who dribbled it up to Nadia.

Alex was sad and confused. She went through the motions of playing the game, but her mind was whirling.

Was her team ignoring her? How was she going to prove that she was a team player if they wouldn't pass to her? Alex could feel sweat collecting on her forehead, and not just because of the heat of the day.

Tweeet! The ref blew his whistle. "That's half time!" he shouted.

Alex headed for the sidelines with relief. Maybe everything would get cleared up during the break.

CHAPTER SEVEN

THE SILENT TREATMENT

"Okay, team. Nice work so far," Manager Mike said, gathering the team into a huddle. "The defence is a little odd."

Alex saw him glance at her with a puzzled look, but she looked away. The manager went on, "But we're playing well. Keep it up!"

"Strikers!" the players yelled as they broke huddle. They scattered to grab their water bottles before the break ended.

Alex looked around for Lin, only to see her friend disappearing into the bathroom. The rest of the players were gathered in little groups, chatting and resting.

No one was talking to Alex. Finally, she couldn't stand the awkwardness one more second.

"Hey, that centre is big, huh?" she said to Christie, trying to sound casual.

Christie looked up from relacing her boots, saw that Alex was speaking to her, then very pointedly looked away without answering.

Alex's face turned bright red. She looked over at Brooke, who was standing nearby, but Brooke looked away also. Alex got the hint. They were all giving her the silent treatment.

She was still being punished for her one little mistake. That's why no one would pass to her. And not even Lin was here to help her out.

Alex felt helpless. Everyone was staring at her with mean looks. Only Manager Mike was oblivious, talking with some parent over by the stands.

Alex thought she'd never felt so alone. Just then, she saw Lin coming back over to the sidelines. She smiled hopefully at her friend. But Lin looked away, too.

Alex couldn't take it anymore. She felt her throat swell and tears spill from her eyes, pouring down her cheeks. She spun on her heel and ran away.

CHAPTER EIGHT

SLURPEE SURPRISE

Alex ran past the car park and through the quiet streets. She was sobbing so hard, she could hardly see. The houses on either side flashed by in a watery blur. Her boots clacked on the sidewalk.

Finally, her sobs slowed and she stopped near a low wall in a garden. She laid her head down on her knees. Her mum had been wrong. Playing hard and playing fair wasn't enough – at least not for her.

Alex got up and wandered down the pavement. She didn't have anywhere to go. She couldn't go back to the game, not after running off the field like that. And she couldn't go home until the game was supposed to be over.

She dragged her feet along the pavement until she came to the corner, where a small corner shop stood. After her horrible day, she decided she could use a treat.

In the reflection of the glass window, she saw a figure approach. Alex swung around. Manager Mike was standing there, his hands in his jacket pockets, smiling.

Alex stepped backwards in surprise. She didn't know what to say. "Sir! What are you doing here?" she spluttered.

"Thirsty?" Manager Mike replied.

He didn't act like there was anything unusual about a manager leaving his team in the middle of a game.

"Uh. . ." Alex stammered.

But the manager already had his hand on the metal push bar of the door. "Wait here," he instructed, pointing to a green bench nearby.

Alex sank down on the bench. When she looked up a minute later, Manager Mike was standing in front of her, holding two giant cherry cokes.

"So," he said, handing her a coke and sitting down beside her on the bench. "What's the trouble?"

"Uh, Sir? Who's coaching the game?" Alex asked.

Her drink was freezing her hands, so she took a mouthful and set it down beside her.

"Oh, that!" Manager Mike said. He waved his hand. "I handed the reins to Brooke's father for a few minutes. He's been trying to get my job all season anyway." He eyed Alex over the drink can. "All joking aside, I can see you're having trouble with the team."

"Is it that obvious?" Alex joked weakly. She felt a wave of shame rise up in her throat. It was bad enough that the other players hated her. But to have the manager know about it somehow seemed worse.

Manager Mike nodded. "You think I spend all of my time staring at that clipboard?" he asked. "Alex, I bet it wasn't easy, moving here in the middle of the school year and leaving your friends behind."

Alex nodded, the familiar lump rising in her throat again.

Manager Mike continued, "It may be selfish of me, but I was glad you joined the Strikers, even if you did have to leave your old team. You're a great midfielder. Tall, strong and quick."

He held up his hand as Alex's mouth opened to respond. "I know you played attacker on your old team," he said, "and I'm sure you were great as a forward. But I don't think that was the right spot for you." He looked right at Alex. "I need you at defence."

Alex nodded. Her old manager had never told her she was needed before. It was nice, feeling needed. "But Sir," she said. "I don't know how I can play if everyone hates me."

Manager Mike stood up and flipped his can into a bin with one decisive gesture. "Nobody hates you, Alex," he said, smiling at her. "They just don't know you. There's only one way to make this whole thing better, and I think you know what you need to do."

Alex looked up. "Isn't it a little too late to apologise to the team?" she asked hesitantly, almost hoping there would be a different answer.

Manager Mike shook his head and looked at his watch. "It's never too late," he said. "I know you didn't mean to score for the other team. Mistakes happen. But it would really make everyone feel better if you just said those two magic words."

"I know, I know," Alex said.

"Come on. Game's almost over. Now's the perfect time," he said, turning and jogging back in the direction of the field.

Alex watched until he was a few streets away, then rose slowly and followed. He was right. It was now or never.

CHAPTER NINE

HARD TO SAY

Alex walked slowly back up the street, through the car park, and to the edge of the field. From where she was standing, she could see that the game must have just ended. The Strikers were scattered on the sidelines, taking off their boots and talking.

Alex stood still, twisting her fingers. The last thing in the world she wanted to do was apologise, but Manager Mike was already waving her over.

There's no way out, she told herself. *You have to do it.*

Alex felt her legs move across the soft turf as if they were moving on their own. One by one, her teammates turned to face her, their eyes curious. She saw Lin standing over to the side. Was it just Alex's imagination, or did Lin look hopeful?

The talking died down and the players fell silent. Manager Mike stepped up next to Alex and laid a hand on her shoulder.

"Listen up, please," he said. "Alex would like to tell all of us something. I'd like you all to listen to her with respect." He gave Alex's shoulder a firm pat and stepped back.

Alex stood alone in front of the sea of watching eyes. Her stomach was churning.

Please, please don't let me throw up, she prayed silently.

Then she caught Lin's sympathetic face, and her friend gave her an encouraging nod.

Alex's stomach steadied itself. She opened her mouth and somehow, the words started coming out.

"Um," she started. "I just wanted to say that . . . I know you all are really mad at me. I'm sorry for scoring that own goal the other day."

She looked at their faces. Brooke and Christie looked suspicious. Alex knew she needed to say more. She shifted her weight.

Her palms were clammy, and she could feel a trickle of sweat running down the side of her face.

"I'm new here," Alex went on, "and everyone already knew each other. I just wanted to help the team. Maybe I was trying too hard. I'm sorry about that. I didn't want to be a ball hog or mess everything up." The words seemed to be getting easier now. At the back, near the stands, she could see Manager Mike, smiling and nodding encouragingly.

"But most of all," Alex went on. "I'm sorry I didn't say sorry earlier." She paused. "Does that make sense?"

A couple of the girls, including Brooke, nodded.

"I don't know why I didn't," Alex added, "except that sorry is hard to say. I know I haven't started out well, but I'm going to try to do better." She stopped talking. No one moved.

The only sounds were distant traffic and a bird singing in a nearby tree. Alex's heart sank. Was this all a mistake? Did they all still hate her?

Then from the back of the group, came the sound of clapping. Alex craned her neck.

Lin and Manager Mike were both applauding, big smiles on their faces. Then the applause spread through the rest of the group.

Brooke, Nadia and Christie were all smiling. And Alex couldn't help smiling back.

"Thanks, guys," she whispered. She didn't think anyone heard her, but Lin pushed her way through the crowd and grabbed Alex up in a hug.

"We're happy to have you on our team," said Brooke.

"Really?" Alex asked.

"Really," Brooke said. "Now, enough talking, let's celebrate our latest win!"

ABOUT THE AUTHOR

Emma Carlson Berne has written more than a dozen books for children and young adults, including teen romance novels, biographies and history books. She lives in Cincinnati, Ohio, USA, with her husband, Aaron, her son, Henry and her dog, Holly.

ABOUT THE ILLUSTRATOR

Katie Wood fell in love with drawing when she was very small. Since graduating from Loughborough University School of Art and Design in 2004, she has been living her dream working as a freelance illustrator. From her studio in Leicester, England, she creates bright and lively illustrations for books and magazines all over the world.

GLOSSARY

ATTACK team that is attacking or trying to score, or the players whose job it is to score

CENTRE one of the players whose job is to score points

DEFENDER person playing defence, trying to keep the other team from scoring

DEFENCE team or players that are trying to prevent the other side from scoring

FORWARD part of the attack; responsible for most of the scoring

GOALIE person who guards the goal and prevents the other team from scoring

INTERCEPTED stole the ball

MIDFIELDER part of the defence; they help with ball control and passing

OFFSIDE penalty when a player has moved ahead of the ball

PENALTY punishment that a team suffers for breaking the rules

SCRIMMAGED played a game for practice, usually between members of the same team

COMPREHENSION QUESTIONS

1. After Alex scored a goal for the other team, the other girls were mad. However, they weren't mad about the goal. They were mad that Alex didn't apologise for her mistake. Do you think they had a right to be mad? Why or why not?

2. Were you surprised that Manger Mike left the game to help Alex? If you were the manager, would you have done the same thing? Explain your answer.

3. Why do you think it was so hard for Alex to apologise to her teammates?

WRITING PROMPTS

1. After the big loss, Manager Mike gave the team a little pep talk. Write your own pep talk to make the Strikers feel better.

2. Would you rather be a defensive player or an attacking player? Write a paragraph explaining your answer.

3. How do you think the Strikers ended the season? Did they lose in the first round of playoffs? Did they win the league? Write a small article for the school newspaper about the Strikers' season.

FOOTBALL FUN

In the United States, the sport is called SOCCER. Nearly everywhere else in the world, fans call it FOOTBALL. Football is the world's most popular sport.

A **NEW BALL** is designed for every World Cup, which takes place every four years. Billions of people around the world watch the World Cup.

The Romans played a game called HARPASTUM. This is said to be the beginning of football in the modern era. However, the origins of football can be traced back more than 2,000 years to China.

ABBY WAMBACH holds the record for most international goals by a male or female player. She had **184** goals in world games in her career.

CRISTIANO RONALDO is one of the most famous and highest-paid football players in the world. He makes over $17 **MILLION** a year.

BRAZIL has won five World Cups, which is the most in the world (1958, 1962, 1970, 1994 and 2002).

KRISTINE LILLY of the United States has played in more football games than any other man or woman in the world. She played in 352 matches before she retired.

GIRLS

with

GAME

SPORT STORIES

HORSEBACK Hurdles

SPORT STORIES

Gymnastics JITTERS

SPORT STORIES

Running Scared

SPORT STORIES

Cheer CHALLENGE

SPORT STORIES

FOOTBALL SURPRISE

SPORT STORIES

DANCE DILEMMA

Read more
SPORT STORIES

THE FUN DOESN'T STOP HERE!

Discover more
Sport Stories at

www.raintree.co.uk